COLLECTOR OF SAND AND TEARS

FORGOTTEN GODS: ORIGINS

LAURA GREENWOOD

Visit Laura Greenwood's website at:

www.authorlauragreenwood.co.uk

Cover by Ravenborn Designs

Collector Of Sand And Tears is a work of fiction. Names, characters, places, and incidents are the products of the author's imagination or are used fictitiously. Any resemblance to actual persons, living or dead, businesses, companies, events, or locales is entirely coincidental.

If you find an error, you can report it via my website: https://www.authorlauragreenwood.co.uk/p/report-error.html

To keep up to date with new releases, sales, and other updates, you can join my mailing list via my website or The Paranormal Council Reader Group on Facebook.

BLURB

Despite her self-imposed exile, the gods want the Eye of Ra back.

But Nehmetawy doesn't want to be used as a weapon anymore and wants to stay free. When Thoth turns up to try and charm her into returning, she's determined to resist his advances.

Soon their conversations lead to more, and neither of them are able to ignore the connection between them.

~

Collector of Sand and Tears is a Forgotten Gods: Origins story which features Nehmetawy and Thoth. It is based on the Ancient Egyptian myth of The Distant Goddess and mythology surrounding the Eye of Ra.

A NOTE ON THE GODS & GODDESSES OF THE FORGOTTEN GODS UNIVERSE

Due to the span of Ancient Egyptian history, many gods and goddesses took on multiple roles over the span of time (as demonstrated in The Queen Of Gods Mini-Series by Hathor's multitude of aspects). In most cases, the gods and goddesses in the fictional Forgotten Gods Universe have been given one of their various aspects. The family links the Ancient Egyptians formed between their gods weren't meant to represent blood family, but aspect ties. This is why many of the gods and goddesses are consorts with their siblings. In the context of the Forgotten Gods Universe, none of the gods are related to one another by blood, but many choose to create family bonds.

You can see a full list of Gods & Goddesses in

the Forgotten Gods Universe, as well as other definitions and information, on my website.

PROLOGUE

I DIDN'T HAVE A NAME. And no one was going to give me one. I was a tool to be used, not someone who deserved to have their own identity.

But there was nothing I could do about it. I was bonded to Ra in a way no one else was. As far as I knew, he wasn't even aware that I had thoughts of my own. It probably wasn't his fault. I didn't have a conventional form, mostly because I didn't dare to take one, I had no idea what would happen if I did.

So I just kept on existing. Doing what Ra said whenever he wanted to smite some humans who didn't do as he commanded. It wasn't something I ever enjoyed, and if I could get away with not doing it, then I would.

But crossing Ra was a bad idea. Nut and Geb had done it not long ago, and ended up cursed for their troubles. There were rumours he planned to do the same with Sekhmet too, who he liked to use in a similar way to me.

Everyone was at his mercy, and he loved the power trip. One day, I was certain he'd lose his title as the first and foremost god. Already I heard mutterings about people shifting their allegiance to Amun and Osiris. If we weren't careful, we were going to end up at war with one another. I wouldn't like to take a bet on who would win. Ra, if he used me. But if I refused and sided with one of his enemies, I could change the tide of everything.

The echo of a smile travelled through me at the thought of how much power that meant I had. Though not a real smile. That would include having a corporeal form when Ra wasn't commanding me to be one.

The door creaked open, drawing my attention away from my thoughts.

It was time to do Ra's bidding.

"There you are," he said curtly, as if he hadn't expected me to be where he'd left me.

Ra's imposing form filled the cold stone room I called home. It was something to do with the way he held himself, his back ramrod straight and his gaze piercing as if he knew everyone's secrets.

He didn't know mine. I'd never let him see what I could feel.

"I have a task for you."

Obviously. He wouldn't be gracing me with his presence if he didn't want something. It never crossed his mind that I might desire some company once in a while.

"You're to go South to Napata and smite those who refuse to do my bidding." He turned around and walked away, not waiting for me to confirm his instructions in any way.

I supposed I'd never given him a reason to doubt I'd fulfil them.

I summoned my magic and prepared myself for the journey to Napata. As the city furthest to the south, it would take a while for me to get there, even with the magic I had flowing through me.

I left the room and flung myself into the sky, taking on the form of a crane as I did. No one would think twice if they looked up and saw me. They wouldn't shout and exclaim that one of the gods was blessing them with their presence. I doubted any of the humans knew I existed beyond that I was the Eye of Ra. The tool he used to scare them even if he wasn't around.

I pushed the bitter thoughts to the side and focused my attention on enjoying the sense of freedom. While I wasn't going to enjoy smiting anyone, I loved travelling. It gave me a chance to take in the lush green banks of the Nile, and the stark contrast where it met the desert sands. Without the river, the country would be nothing. Thankfully, Taweret and Sobek did their part to make sure the annual flood came and went at the right time, making the land fertile and the people prosperous.

And in Napata, I was going to destroy that.

What if I didn't this time?

I could keep on going. It would be a while before Ra realised I wasn't coming back, and what was he going to do if I didn't? He might send a search party after me, but I was powerful enough to be certain I could hide myself away. No one would have the ability to force me either.

I could be free. I wasn't sure what I'd do with that freedom, but so long as it was something that wasn't destroying lives and being forced to collect the tears of Ra's enemies, it would be good for me.

Napata rose in front of me before I was ready for it to. The idea of heading down onto the city and taking on a more menacing form filled me with dread. I didn't want to hurt anyone. I never had on my own terms, and I was tired of doing someone else's bidding. I deserved to be my own person as much as everyone else did.

Without even realising what I was doing, I sped past Napata, not losing any height. For a moment, I faltered. I had no idea if there would be any consequences to me ignoring my instructions. Magic could be a fickle thing, for all I knew, I might drop out of the sky now I'd decided not to do as Ra commanded.

But I didn't. I kept on flying past the boundaries of Egypt and beyond. The desert sands called to me. No one would think to look for me there. Who would want to live in a place without water or greenery?

It was a good trade if I got to be free for the first time in my life.

ONE

GODS HAVE COME AND GONE. Each of them was sent by Ra for the express purpose of persuading me to return to Karnak and his control.

Most of the time, I'd managed to avoid them completely, but in some cases, they'd found me and tried to command me to return.

That had gotten them an earful. I wasn't going to be beholden to anyone ever again, especially not Ra.

I transformed myself into a graceful lioness. If I felt like grandstanding, I'd say it was because I was ferocious and untameable, but in reality, it was mostly because no one around here would dare approach a lion on their own. A group of people big enough to take on a lion would be easy for me to hear coming and get away from.

Which made it the perfect disguise to be roaming around in.

The sun beat down on my golden coat, warming me through. I'd need to find shelter before the hottest part of the day, even magic couldn't save me from the burning heat. Well, it probably could. But I wasn't about to risk it. If I got sick or otherwise damaged myself beyond repair, then I was going to have to go back to Karnak with my tail between my legs whether I wanted to or not.

I wasn't about to let that happen.

The desert heat began to get to me. I slunk off back to the cave I'd made into my home. Not that there was a lot there. But it was mine and no one else knew about it. Just the way I liked it.

The scuffing of leather against stone reached my ears as I approached my cave. I froze, the fur all over my body standing on end. I wasn't sure whether that was a magical reaction, or one that mirrored the way a lion would respond to someone being in their territory. It probably didn't matter. Whatever the reason, I could sense there was someone in my space who shouldn't be there.

I let out a loud growl. It would scare away whatever approaching human was brave enough to try and disturb me.

The footsteps continued.

Great. I was going to have to try even harder.

I increased my size to make myself even more imposing.

A man strode into view without a care in the world. He didn't act as if he was coming into a lion's den, even though I was reasonably sure he could see me.

"Hello," he said.

I glare at him, recognising the handsome features as those belonging to the god of wisdom.

I shouldn't be surprised Ra had started to send the more important and powerful gods to come collect me. What I was surprised about was that someone like Thoth would come.

"You weren't very easy to find," he said as he sat down on a boulder.

The remains of my fire sat between us. I should have thought about hiding that better. Nothing said not a real lion like having made a fire when I had no hands. I supposed it was too late to worry about that now. The damage was already done.

I cocked my head to the side. Did he think I wanted to be found? The whole point of coming this far away from home and hanging out in the desert with no one around was so that people wouldn't disturb me.

Thoth chuckled and opened his pack, pulling out

a jar. From the smell, it held wine. What I wouldn't give to drink some of it. "Yes, I get it, I know that's the point."

Oops. I hadn't meant to project my thoughts. Too much time alone had made me lapse at not doing that.

"I've been instructed to bring you back to Karnak."

I'm not going. This time, I did mean to let him sense my thoughts. As far as I was aware, they didn't come across as words, just as the vague impression of the thoughts.

"I thought you might say that."

Then you can pack up and go tell Ra as much.

He raised an eyebrow. "You don't know me."

Correct. What's your point?

"That I'm not going to give up so easily."

A wave of amusement passed through me. So you've seen what Ra does to the people who fail.

"I have," he admitted. "But how do you know, you haven't been back to Karnak in months?"

Call it an educated guess, you aren't the only smart person in this cave.

"I didn't think I was. You were clever enough to get around the containment spell Ra placed on you."

There was no need, he sent me on an assignment.

Thoth raised an eyebrow. "And you really think that was enough to break free of him? You have more power than you know."

Hmm. Maybe he had a point. I'd thought about flying away before, but I'd never managed to go through with it. Perhaps there was something in what he was saying, though I honestly had no idea what.

He got to his feet and dusted himself down. "Anyway, I'm going to find myself a place to stay. I don't want to seem like a rude guest, but your cave is lacking some of the comforts I've become used to."

Sorry it couldn't be more accommodating.

"Are you?"

Not in the slightest. I don't want to encourage unwelcome visitors to overstay.

He dipped his head in response. "Message received. I'll leave you to the rest of your day."

His return the next day was promised in the words he didn't say. I chose not to comment on it. He'd do whatever it was he'd come here to do, I'd refuse to go with him, and then he'd return to Karnak and leave me to my peaceful life in Punt.

After he'd gone, I was sure he'd be replaced by a new messenger. And when he was, I'd deal with that poor god or goddess. I knew it wasn't really their fault. They were as stuck in Ra's thrall as I had been, and I couldn't blame anyone for that when it had taken me so long to break free.

TWO

I CLAMBERED over the rocks and to the ridge I liked to sit on while I watched the world pass me by. It was early in the day still, and the rocks were pleasantly warm from the heat of the sun.

I laid down and put my head on my paws, letting my eyes fall closed as I basked.

There was no doubt in my mind that Thoth would be back today, and I wanted to make the most of the time I had without him bothering me.

The crunch of stones alerted me to his arrival. It had taken him less time than I'd expected for him to find me. Maybe I should have hidden myself better, but if I was honest, I wanted this over sooner rather than later. Most of the gods Ra sent barely lasted a couple of days before they gave up. There was no reason for me to suppose he was going to be any different. At some point, Ra was going to have to get bored of sending people after me. While they were here, they weren't doing whatever it is they were supposed to back at Karnak. I couldn't imagine him being particularly happy with that. I wasn't worth enough to want back forever.

"Good morning." He sat down beside me and leaned back against the rock.

I opened an eye, but didn't move any more than that.

"Can I tell you a story?"

I made a non-committal noise that was something between a purr and a growl. He was easy to listen to, and it had been lonely to have so much time alone. Not that I'd had much company even before I'd come to Punt, but at least there had been other people for me to listen to there.

But I also didn't want him to think that I was coming around to his way of thinking. I wasn't planning on going back to Karnak no matter what happened.

"All right. Do you have any preference?"

No.

I didn't know any stories. It would be interesting to hear him tell me one.

"There was a king who lived in the middle of nowhere with his wife and daughter he loved very much. But before the princess reached adulthood, her mother grew very sick and passed away..."

That's not a very happy start to a story.

"It has a happy ending," Thoth promised me.

We'll see.

He didn't say anything about me interrupting him, which was probably a good thing. I didn't imagine this would be the last time I did that.

"The king was saddened by his wife's passing, and mourned her like he should by visiting her tomb. But after a year, he grew lonely..."

Only a year? That isn't very long if she was the love of his life.

"I don't know if she was," Thoth responded. "Maybe he married her for the wrong reasons."

The poor woman.

"Indeed. I'm sure she would have preferred a life with love."

Wouldn't we all?

"Yes," he agreed, a sadness entering his tone.

Before I could ask him to elaborate, he cleared his throat to continue his tale.

"One day, the king met a matchmaker, and the two discussed a second marriage. The king took an anklet from his deceased wife and declared the woman who it fit would be his new wife."

I can't say that's a very good criterion for marriage.

"I don't think it's supposed to be."

Ah, so you're not telling me a romantic story?

"It has romantic elements."

I cocked my head to the side, which probably wasn't anywhere near as expressive when it was coming from a lion. But I had no human form, just like I had no name. Both would be useful in this situation.

I pushed the thought aside. Why would I want to be human around Thoth?

He was unsurprisingly oblivious to my thoughts, and continued on with his story.

"Despite searching throughout the land, the matchmaker couldn't find a woman the anklet would fit, but even so, she refused to tell anyone that the man in question was the king."

That seems like a recipe for disaster.

He shot me a knowing look. Hmm. Perhaps I'd stumbled upon an important part of the story.

"The matchmaker finally came across the princess while she was going about her day. She offered her the anklet and it fit perfectly. The princess was excited, thinking fate had intervened and found her a husband..."

I wrinkled my nose. It wasn't going to be fun for

the princess to find out she was supposed to marry her father.

"The night before the wedding arrived, and the princess still had no idea who she had agreed to marry. Nervous, she talked to the daughter of the minister, going as far as to bribe her with a golden bangle. The girl told the princess the truth about her bridegroom. The princess was horrified..."

Rightly so.

Thoth nodded. "...and she sent everyone away so she could escape. She headed to the tanner and paid him a handful of coins to make her a suit of leather that would cover her from head to toe. She dressed herself in rags and pretended to be a beggar woman roaming around the grounds."

I would too, if my father wanted to marry me.

Thoth chuckled. "Do you have a father?"

You know the answer to that question.

"I know that you technically don't have one. But I know several gods and goddesses who choose to call one another by family names. I didn't know if you had someone you considered to be your father."

I suppose it would be Ra in the conventional sense.

"Gods aren't conventional," Thoth pointed out.

Neither are the humans in your story.

He let out a soft laugh. "I haven't got to the end, yet."

Then you should continue. I wanted to hear the end, and had to hope things would work out for the princess.

He took a sip of water from the jar he'd brought with him. "Once it was time for the wedding, the king entered the bridal chamber and found it empty. He sent his guards to search the palace to find his bride, and discovered his daughter was also missing."

Ah, so he didn't know he was supposed to marry his own daughter.

"Wait and see," Thoth responded. "The princess came across soldiers at the gate and they asked her if she'd seen the king's daughter. She replied that her name was Juleidah, and she had not, describing herself as the old beggar woman she appeared to be. Once she left the palace, she ran until she was too tired to continue on, having reached a neighbouring kingdom."

Poor Juleidah.

"A slave girl came upon her and called for her queen. Once Juleidah was awake, they asked her who she was, and she repeated the same refrain she'd given to her father's guards. The queen invited her inside the palace to join the slaves and servants,"

Thoth continued. "But Juleidah caught the eye of the queen's son."

She hasn't caught a break, has she?

Thoth chuckled. "I guess not."

What happened next? I shuffled closer so I could catch every word he said.

To his credit, he barely responded to my move.

"Unlike before, when the prince asked Juleidah where she came from, she told him the truth and the prince decided he would travel there. While he wasn't paying attention, Juleidah took the ring from the prince's hand."

I frowned. Why would she do that?

"Juleidah went to the kitchens of the palace and asked if she could help prepare food, but the cook was reluctant. After a while, she was given some dough. She shaped it and placed the ring inside. Once the bread was baked, she packed it with the prince's things. He set out on his journey, but when he found the ring, he ordered everyone to return to the palace. After he returned, he and Juleidah got married."

That's a strange jump to go from a ring in some bread to marriage.

Thoth shrugged. "It isn't my story, I'm just the teller."

That doesn't mean it shouldn't make sense.

"Maybe the prince took it as a sign that he should be with Juleidah?"

A sign she created. It was hard not to scoff at the turn of events, but he was right. He was just telling the story.

"Back in Juleidah's father's palace, the matchmaker had been put in chains, the king very unhappy with the chain of events. He searched everywhere for his bride and his daughter, still believing the matchmaker had made both disappear and not realising they were the same person. Eventually, he came across the palace where Juleidah now lived with her prince. She invited him inside and gave them food, drink, and a place to sleep. Once her visitors had their fill, she revealed her identity to her father, and told him the entire story."

I bet he got a surprise.

"He did," Thoth agreed. "He was so angry with the matchmaker for her deceit, that he ordered her to be thrown into the ravine as punishment."

That might be a little harsh.

He raised an eyebrow. "Haven't you done worse to people Ra has ordered you to smite?"

I flicked my tail back and forth, annoyance simmering within me.

"I'm sorry, I didn't mean it that way."

I know. My terseness came through my thoughts if the set of his jaw was anything to go by.

"And that is the tale of the princess in the suit of leather," he finished. "Juleidah's father was happy to know his daughter was safe, and gifted half of his kingdom to her, allowing them all to live happily together."

I raised an eyebrow. Or tried to.

That's a surprisingly happy ending for a story that started with death.

"Death is just a beginning, you know that."

Not one we'll ever experience.

"True. It is something for humans and not us."

Does that make you sad?

"Sometimes," he admitted. "You?"

I shook my head from side to side. There are things I lament more than the inability to die.

"Like?"

Not being able to be my own person.

"You can change that," he whispered, his words carried by the wind. "If you want to."

I wasn't so sure about that. But I guessed only time would tell.

THREE

I WASN'T sure how many days and nights it had been. I stopped counting after fifty. I wasn't sure why Thoth hadn't given up yet. He was determined, I had to give him that. Of course, that only led to another question.

Why was I letting him come back day after day when I had no intention of giving in to him?

If I was feeling kind to myself, I liked the idea that Ra was having to struggle through ruling his domain without someone as important as Thoth by his side. If I was being more honest, I liked his company. There was something about sitting side by side while he told me about things that happened between the other gods at Karnak, or stories of a time even earlier than ours.

A small part of me didn't want it to end, though I knew it had to.

I wasn't about to mention it to Thoth, though.

A gentle breeze brushed past my fur, bringing the scent of the man sitting next to me.

Well, god. He wasn't a mere mortal by any stretch of the imagination, even if he chose to take the form of one while with me. He could take another form if he wished.

I had to wonder about his choice of an ibis though, was there any particular reason for that? Perhaps in time, he'd tell me. He'd covered a lot of other topics since we'd met, but his own preferences hadn't come up much.

"You need to return to Karnak," Thoth said, pulling my thoughts away from how much I liked to spend time with him.

I let out a low rumble akin to a growl. I could have used my thoughts, but I didn't trust myself not to say something I didn't mean.

He didn't take the warning for what it was. That was foolish of him. I was giving him the chance to rethink what he was saying.

"Each of us was created for a reason. We're needed in order to maintain the balance and justice for the world. Every god or goddess has a purpose they were designed to fulfil, and that includes you."

I flicked my tail in annoyance. I was well aware of what I'd been created for. What he didn't seem to understand was that I didn't want to do it. I supposed in some ways, it made sense that he didn't get it. He was the god of wisdom and knowledge. They weren't bad things and his purpose wasn't to explicitly hurt people.

Mine was. And that made things different. How was I supposed to accept that I had to do my duty and not listen to the way I felt when I was supposed to destroy things.

"Without you, the balance isn't in place like it should be and that's causing problems you can't imagine."

I chuffed. I could imagine them. It wasn't about balance, it was about Ra's power and I wasn't foolish enough to believe otherwise. I was surprised Thoth was so easily taken in. He was supposed to think in such a way that he didn't need to be told these things.

My tail flicked back and forth in frustration. How was I supposed to let my feelings be known when I couldn't say a word.

Yet another thing to curse Ra for. He'd never intended me to be able to think, so hadn't given me a way to express myself.

Except maybe that wasn't true. I wasn't

supposed to be able to think for myself, but I could. Maybe that meant I would be able to talk if I tried to.

I opened my mouth to try and force the words out. Unsurprisingly, a loud roar was all I managed. It thundered through the surrounding area and vibrated through me. My pent up rage echoed through the sound.

"Are you all right?" Thoth asked.

Instead of soothing me, his question only made me angrier. I wanted to shout and scream at him to point out that I was very much not all right, and it was partly his fault.

Something shifted inside me, but I wasn't sure what it was. Something was clawing and trying to push its way free.

I gave in. Not that I had much choice. Whatever was happening within me had control, I probably wouldn't have been able to stop it even if I'd wanted to.

My form seemed to increase in size, something I didn't think I was capable of. As far as I was aware, I could take the form of a select number of animals, but the size wasn't something I was capable of altering.

I was being proved wrong. My rebellious

expedition to Punt was certainly teaching me some new things about myself.

Fire raged in my belly, urging me to let it free.

I opened my mouth, thinking it was anger wanting me to express myself again, but I was badly mistaken. Red hot flames spurted from me, scorching the stones around me and turning the already hot desert even hotter.

Thoth screeched from beside me as he shifted into the form of an ibis and darted into the air. I imagined it would probably be uncomfortable for him to be flying in the midday sun, but I supposed it wasn't nearly as bad as being burned by fire when he wasn't able to die.

I wasn't particularly inclined to hang around either.

I snapped my jaw shut and leapt from the rocky shelf we'd been sitting on with no real care for how far down it was. I knew the form I was currently in could survive the jump, even if I didn't really understand why any of this was happening.

My paws barely stayed on the ground long enough for the hot sand to start to burn as I darted towards my cave.

It was only as I approached that I realised I hadn't actually told Thoth no about going back to Karnak. He'd probably gotten the message when I started trying to burn everything around us. Despite his blindness over Ra and what his motivations were, he wasn't a dumb man.

The flames had cooled the anger inside me, and even though I had wanted to get away from Thoth and his insistence on my return to Karnak, I didn't want to reject him as much as I had without explaining why. The most probable reason for his lack of knowledge about Ra and how he treated me was that no one had ever told him. Which meant I needed to. If he understood, perhaps he'd finally accept that my answer was no for good.

Which meant it was time for me to learn how to talk.

FOUR

I'D NEVER FELT as nervous as this before, but as I returned to the ledge, it was almost impossible to control.

What if I'd scared Thoth away? While I was still frustrated with him for trying to lecture me into returning to Karnak, I'd enjoyed spending time with him over the past couple of months, and didn't want that to end.

My heart sank when I approached and found the ledge completely empty.

I'd scared him away.

The early morning warmth wasn't as comforting as normal. I flopped down onto the surface and closed my eyes. I hated how much I cared about him not being here. Especially after I'd spent the night practising how to talk out loud to surprise him. I'd never realised I was able to until now.

The scuff boots against rock reached me. My ears pricked and I lifted my head. Was it Thoth, or was it just another human heading this way?

Relief flooded through me the moment I spied Thoth's familiar face popping up over the ridge.

He'd come back.

I couldn't explain the way I felt, or why it was so strong within me. Maybe it was just because I was starting to see him as a friend. I'd never had one before. Which made sense. None of the other gods who had come to try and convince me to return had bothered trying to have a conversation with me.

"Hello," he said as he took a seat beside me.

Good morning. I hadn't meant to use my thoughts, but they'd just slipped out.

"I feel like we got off on the wrong foot," he said slowly.

I cocked my head to the side and waited for him to continue.

"What's your name?"

I blinked a couple of times. Wasn't he aware that I didn't have one?

He nodded, understanding seeming to have dawned on him. "When I first came into being, I didn't have a name either. Whenever anyone asked me what it was, I'd just stand there, completely bewildered."

"But you know everything," I said, taking him by surprise by the word being spoken out loud.

Thoth chuckled, a rich sound that I was coming to like, whether I wanted to or not. "I don't know how to convince you to come back to Karnak."

"That's because you've only asked me three-hundred-and-sixteen times."

"Will the three-hundred-and-seventeenth time do the trick?"

"It won't," I said decisively.

"I didn't think so, but it was worth a try." He sighed and leaned back against the rock.

I laid down and rested my head against my front paws.

"Will you ever show me your human form?" he asked.

"I don't have one." I closed my eyes and let the sun warm my fur. If I went back, I'd miss being able to do this. To take pleasure in the way the heat of the day travelled through me and welcomed me with open arms.

I side-eyed Thoth. I'd miss sitting with him too. His stories might have started out as a mild irritant, but I was coming to enjoy the way he wove them. So long as he didn't start lecturing me again.

"You have a human form," he assured me. "We all do."

"I've never found it."

"Is that because Ra told you not to?"

I tilted my head and considered whether that was true. "I suppose."

Thoth sighed. "I think you're a little bit beyond doing what Ra says."

I chuffed, a sound that I figured replaced a chuckle while I was in this form. "That's true. The others said he's angry with me. Well, they shouted it at me from across the sand. They didn't really tell me anything."

"I'm sure they said a lot of things," Thoth muttered. "I don't think angry is the right word. He's scared."

"Of me?"

"If I'm honest, I don't know. Perhaps a little bit. But mostly, I think he's scared about what will happen to him if he doesn't have you to frighten others with."

I sighed. "I hope you don't think that's going to convince me to come back."

"I don't. But maybe something to think about is whether or not you could come back and leverage that."

"I still can't believe he sent someone as

important as you to do something as simple as collect me," I observed.

"Maybe I'm not as important as you think I am."

"You're the god of wisdom, aren't you?"

He chuckled. "I think it's punishment for the help I gave Nut and Geb," he admitted. "He didn't say as much, but that's because he's never had any proof it was me who did."

My lips twisted into the approximation of a smile. Now Thoth had mentioned a human form, I was finding the feline one even more limiting than I normally did.

"Why did you help them?"

"How could I not? Nut was already pregnant, she couldn't stay that way forever."

"That's not all there is to it, is it?"

He shook his head. "There are prophecies and predictions about one of the gods she birthed being able to topple Ra."

"Aren't prophecies and predictions the same thing?"

"More or less, but prophecies are more dramatic and vague."

I chuffed. "Then I think I prefer predictions."

"Me too."

"It was nice of you to help them," I said.

"Thank you. It was the right thing to do."

"I hope these prophecies and predictions are right," I admitted. "I don't want Ra to be in power forever."

"He won't be. That's not how the world works. The waves of power will come and go. It might be Ra now, but it might be Osiris next, or Ma'at in the future."

"A goddess? Interesting."

"You seem surprised."

"I didn't think the gods would be ready to take instructions from a goddess." While the goddesses I'd encountered were all just as powerful as their male counterparts in terms of magic, they didn't have quite the same political or social power.

"I don't think they're ready yet," he agreed. "But in the future, I think they will."

"Interesting. And I suppose with your job title, we should expect it to come true."

"Just like you naming yourself will," he agreed.

"I think my name is Nehmetawy." My voice was barely a whisper, but I could already tell that it felt right, even if I had no logical reason to feel that way. I'd never given much thought about what to call myself.

"It's a pleasure to meet you, Nehmetawy," Thoth said.

Oh. I liked it even more when he said it.

"How does it feel?" he asked.

"Like I can finally start to figure out who I am."

A smile crept over his face. "I'm glad I could help."

I was too. Who knew it would take one of Ra's messengers for me to finally be able to start feeling like I was my own person.

FIVE

I BRUSHED my hands down the dress I was wearing. It felt odd against my skin, but I knew I couldn't walk around naked like I was used to doing when I was in a non-human form. I'd been practising moving in human form for a while, but hadn't had the courage to show Thoth how I was doing until now.

The heat felt different on my tanned skin compared to the fur I was used to wearing here in the desert. My lioness' body was definitely more suited to the environment, but I knew this was important.

I climbed up to the ledge, noting how much harder it was on two legs instead of four. I wondered if Thoth transformed into his ibis form to fly over part of it and make things easier for himself. He'd never mentioned it, but I'd never asked.

It took me longer to get to our ledge than it normally would, and Thoth was already seated there when I arrived. He was staring out onto the desert with his back to me.

All right, this was it.

I cleared my throat. "Morning."

He got to his feet and turned around to face me. It took him a moment to process that it was me standing in front of him, but he understood quickly enough.

"Nehmetawy," he whispered. "You look beautiful."

I dipped my head and tucked a strand of dark brown hair behind my ear. "Thank you."

"How long have you been working on this?"

"How long is it since you first came here?" I asked as I went over to join him and the two of us sat down on the rock.

I dangled my feet over the edge for the first time. I had to admit this was fun.

"Seven hundred and fifty-two days," he responded.

I raised an eyebrow. "You've been away from Karnak for over two years."

"So I have."

"Won't they be worrying that you've run away too?"

"I doubt it. Ra told me to take as long as it took. They probably think I'm going to arrive back with you by my side any day now," he said. "Though I don't think it's likely?"

I laughed lightly. "Is that your way of asking today?"

"Yes. It's good to get it out of the way."

He wasn't wrong. He still asked every single day, but I could tell from the way he worded it now that he wasn't as invested in the answer as he used to be.

"I won't be coming back to Karnak with you," I said, turning him down just like I had seven hundred and fifty-one times before.

I hoped he wouldn't get bored. A small pang of guilt travelled through me as I realised I'd kept him away from his duties for so long.

"What are you feeling guilty about?" Thoth asked.

"What?" My voice came out as more of a squeak than before.

"Your expressions are easier to read when you're in this form."

"Oh." I reached up and touched my cheek. "I hadn't thought about that."

"You'll get used to it," he promised. "It suits you."

"I should hope so, this was what my magic wanted me to be."

He nodded. "That's normal."

We slipped into our normal pattern of conversation, without many differences between today and how we usually talked. Though we sat closer together, something I found myself liking more than I wanted to admit.

Before either of us realised what was happening, the sun was starting to set and the cooler night air swept past us.

A shiver ran through me at the drop in temperature. This was the longest I'd been in my human form and I wasn't prepared for it.

Without hesitation, Thoth reached out and put an arm around me.

I stilled for a moment, then shuffled closer, resting my head against his shoulder. Neither of us say anything as we sit there closer than we ever have before.

Something about the way we're sitting together makes me feel far more comfortable than I have ever before, and not just because of the warmth coming from his body.

"Is this all right?" he asked. "You can change

into a different form if you'll be more at ease."

I shook my head. "I'm fine. If you are."

"I don't think I've ever been more fine." His words were faint and almost indiscernible even with the gentle wind.

I had to agree with him. This felt so right.

Which I guessed made sense. We'd been spending every day together for over a year and I still looked forward to our talks. And after so long, I was reasonably sure it was no longer a novelty thing. We were friends. That was the only explanation I could come up with for the way I felt around him.

"Will you come in this form tomorrow?" he asked.

"I think so. I like it more than I expected to." The longer I'd stayed in it, the more familiar it had become.

"A lot of the gods and goddesses who came into existence with a different form have said the same."

"Did it take them a while to find their human form too?" I asked.

"Some of them. If you're worried about the amount of time it took you to find your form, you shouldn't. I've known some people take longer. Apis has yet to find his."

I nodded. "That is reassuring."

"I'm glad." He paused, as if reluctant to say more.

"What is it?"

Thoth sighed. "I don't think you're going to like it..."

"Which means it's about returning to Karnak," I reasoned. "What if I promised not to get annoyed?"

He chuckled. "Do you have the capability when it comes to this?"

"Fine. I can try not to get annoyed."

"I was just going to point out that you could return to Karnak in this form. You can insist on not being treated the same. You've been gone for long enough that you have the upper hand..."

"I'll think about it."

His eyebrows shoot up.

"Not expecting that response?" I teased.

"No."

"Sometimes, I like to take you by surprise."

"You managed."

"Then I succeeded in my plan." Another shiver ran through me as the temperature dropped again.

"We should call it a night," Thoth said. "It's cold and late. But we can talk more tomorrow?"

"Just like every other day," I promised, already looking forward to it.

Each day with Thoth was better than the last.

SIX

MY HUMAN FORM had become more and more comfortable ever since showing it to Thoth. Perhaps it was because I also had a name to go with it. I had an identity, something I truly felt I'd been lacking before.

But one thing was becoming increasingly certain, I couldn't go back to being Ra's attack weapon. No matter what happened, it wasn't an option.

I'd grown increasingly certain Thoth wouldn't let me return to that either. It was reassuring to know I had someone who would watch out for me.

I waited at the bottom of the cliff we normally sat on. I'd asked him to meet me at the bottom instead of on the ledge so I could take him back to my cave and show him where I'd been living. After nearly a thousand days of sitting and talking, it felt right to be sharing where I spent my evenings.

Thoth approached from the left, his face lighting up the moment he saw me. I was certain mine did the same.

"What were you thinking for today?" he asked once he reached me. "This is an unusual meeting place."

"I thought you might like to see my cave. If not, we can..."

"I'd love to," he said quickly.

"Follow me."

Nerves fluttered within my chest as I led him through the maze of passageways through the rocks. This was one of the reasons I'd picked this specific place. The warren made it difficult for people to find me, but also protected me from the sandstorms and other weather anomalies that assaulted the desert from time to time.

"This isn't where I found you on the first day," Thoth observed as we neared the centre of the rocky outcrop.

"I changed the cave I was staying in so you couldn't find me again. In hindsight, there wasn't much need for that, but..."

"You didn't know whether I was just going to be another one of Ra's messengers," he supplied.

"Exactly. I'm sorry for thinking that of you."

"There's nothing to apologise for. I was one of Ra's messengers in the first place, I just got to know you and things changed."

"They did for me too," I agreed. "We're here."

I led him into the space I called home. There wasn't much to it, though I had accumulated a few things over the past few years.

A small fire crackled from near the entrance. Despite the heat of the day, it didn't penetrate this far and I needed something for the warmth.

"It's a lovely space," he said.

"It's a cave," I countered. "But it's home."

I gestured for him to take a seat next to the fire. He did, and lifted up his arms so I could sit next to him.

But something wasn't right about the expression on his face.

"What's wrong?" I asked, settling down next to him and resting my hand on his chest. We'd sat closely like this every day since I'd taken on a human form, but somehow, it felt more intimate now we were in my cave.

"How can you tell something is wrong?"

"The way you're holding yourself. I'm not really sure." I frowned, trying to search for what made me ask.

"Ra sent a messenger for me."

"Did he finally think you'd run away?"

He gave a short laugh, but it wasn't full of the same amusement as normal. "No. He said that I have a hundred more days to bring you back."

"Or what?"

"I honestly don't know."

"You know I have to say no."

"You do realise that if I go back without you, Ra will just send someone else in my place," Thoth said.

"He's tried that. It didn't work."

"He isn't going to stop," Thoth warned. "You know what he's like."

I shrugged. "I'm honestly surprised he still cares. He's survived this long without me smiting his enemies, I'm sure he can last longer."

Thoth chuckled. "I imagine it's more about the principle. He doesn't like being bested."

"Hmm. True."

"But we could find a way that you don't have to do that anymore. It would take some doing, but I think I could convince Ra."

"You would do that for me?" The surprise in my voice is impossible to ignore.

"Of course I would. I'd do anything for you, Nehmetawy. And for your freedom."

I reached out and touched his cheek with my fingers.

He turned to face me, a thousand emotions swimming in his eyes. I didn't need him to say the words out loud to know he didn't want to return to Karnak in a hundred days. He didn't want to leave me.

And I didn't want him to go. I wanted to ask him to stay, but I knew I couldn't do that. He had duties to attend to and I was already keeping him away from them. I knew it was his choice to stay this long, but it didn't help the guilt.

"You're so beautiful," he whispered.

"I could say the same about you."

He leaned in, closing the gap between us. My eyes fluttered closed as his lips brushed against mine.

At first, there was a hesitance to both of our touches, but I felt him relax into it at the same moment I did. There was something magical about the way it felt to kiss him. If I'd known it would be like this, then I would have done this much earlier.

We broke the kiss and pulled away from one another.

"I've wanted to do that for months," he whispered.

"Me too."

"Then aren't we fools?"

A small laugh escaped from me. "Maybe just a little bit. Do you need to be anywhere else tonight?"

He shook his head. "It might surprise you to know you're the only reason I'm in Punt. I've been heading back to a small hut in the evenings and waiting for the sun to rise so I can see you again. There's nothing else for me here but you."

His words sank in, filling me with an intense sense of belonging.

Which was when I realised the only thing keeping me here was him.

What did that mean for my refusal to return to Karnak? If I wanted to spend more time with him, that was where I needed to be.

The idea sat heavily within me. I didn't know if I could go through with it and return. But at least I knew what I had to do if I wanted to stay with him. All that was left was deciding whether I could go through with it.

SEVEN

I SAT at the entrance of the cave, my hands cradling a cup of water as I contemplated the difficult conversation I had to have.

Thoth's hundred days weren't up yet, but it was only a couple of weeks until they were, and I didn't want to leave things until the last minute to talk about this.

"Nehmetawy?" he called from the back of the cave, his voice still thick with sleep.

At least I'd been able to spend more time with him now he didn't have to go back to his hut on an evening. I should have brought him to my cave earlier.

"I'm here," I responded. "There's some fresh bread by the fire for you."

"Thanks."

Even with my back to the cave, I could hear him moving around getting himself some breakfast before he came to join me.

"What's brought you here so early? You only sit like this when you have something hard to think about."

I smiled weakly. "You know me so well."

"It's been a thousand and seventy-seven days," he pointed out. "I'd like to think I know you as well as anyone else does."

"No one has even bothered to try before, you know me the best in the whole world."

"And you know me that way too."

"I don't feel like I do..."

"You should," he countered. "I've shared parts of myself with you that I've never told anyone."

"You've never talked about why your main alternative form is an ibis."

"You've never asked."

"Consider that what I'm doing now."

He chuckled. "My name means he who is like an ibis, so that's what the humans associated me with and what I got the power to turn into. It doesn't feel like a particularly exciting reason when I put it like that."

"Oh."

"You sound disappointed."

"I thought there might be some exciting reason behind it."

"My apologies."

We lapsed into comfortable silence as he ate his breakfast. It had become so normal for the two of us to sit like this, and I welcomed it as the norm.

But I couldn't avoid the conversation forever.

I took a deep breath and steeled my nerves.

"I'm going to come back to Karnak with you," I said, the words coming out as barely more than a soft whisper.

Thoth looked up sharply, almost dropping his cup of water in the process. "Are you sure?"

I nodded.

"But you've been so adamant..."

"And the reasons for that haven't changed. I don't want to be Ra's puppet any more. I don't want to fly around Egypt to destroy lives and property because he thinks the humans there have done something wrong. Especially when I never saw any evidence of wrongdoing."

"But?" A hint of hesitant hope lingered in his voice.

"I don't want you to go and leave me wondering when I'm going to see you again."

"I'd come back to visit," he promised.

"And how often would that be? Every few months? Once a year? Twice a decade?"

"I don't know," he admitted. "But I'd try..."

"That's just it. You shouldn't have to try. If I don't go back to Karnak now, then I can't go back for just a visit. I'd be trapped outside. I don't want to do that to you. And I don't want to give you up," I said.

My heart pounded. I was reasonably sure he felt the same way I did, but there would be no proof of it until he responded to my words.

"Are you saying you want to come back to Karnak just because of me? I can't let you do that." Thoth reached out to take my hand in his and gave it a reassuring squeeze. "As much as I would want you there every day, I don't want it to come at the cost of your freedom."

"But this is about that too," I assured him. "If I want to be able to go about my life the way I want to, then I need to go back to Karnak and make sure that's the case. If I don't..." I trailed off, not wanting to think about the alternative. Until Thoth showed up, I had no real concept of how lonely I'd been.

"I could stay instead," Thoth suggested. "We could roam the world and find some other budding civilisations to be gods to."

I smiled even at his suggestion. It was sweet, but misguided. "You have duties to attend to."

"New gods are coming into being all the time. They can find someone else to fill the role."

"Do you really want that?"

Indecision warred over his face. "Honestly?"

"After nearly three years, I'd expect nothing but honesty," I pointed out.

Thoth sighed, revealing all I needed to know about how he really felt. "No, I don't want someone else to take over my work. I've put so much into it."

I reached out and placed a hand on top of his, giving it a squeeze. "I understand that. And it's one of the reasons I've decided to do this. I don't want you to turn your back on your work for me."

"And you're not just coming back just because I've constantly asked you to?"

"We both know you never asked seriously after the first few weeks." It had become a habit that both of us hadn't thought about much. Or at least, I hadn't.

"True."

"Why did you stay so long?"

Silence fell between us, but I didn't worry about whether or not he'd answer. He would. We'd shared so much of ourselves in the past few years, he wasn't going to shut down on me now.

"I liked the company," he admitted. "Back at Karnak, everyone treats me like the person who has all the answers..."

"You're the god of wisdom, you're supposed to have all the answers."

His lips twisted into a small smile. "Maybe. But it gets tiring after a while."

"So you stayed with me because you wanted a break?"

"I stayed with you because you made me feel like a person and not a god."

"Oh."

"Is that not the answer you wanted?"

"It is," I assured him quickly. "And none of this changes my mind. I want to reclaim my powers and my position without losing the ability to make my own decisions."

Thoth nodded. "All right. We can return to Karnak together, that way you won't have to face what's waiting for you alone."

"Thank you. I'm nervous, but I think it's the right thing to do."

"I know I'll be glad to have you around." He leaned in and placed a soft kiss against my cheek.

"Me too. I haven't wanted to return before because it's always been too overwhelming to think about what waits for me. The worries are still there, but somehow they feel a little bit more manageable. I know I have you to thank for that."

"I'm glad I could be that person for you," Thoth whispered.

"How could you not be? You're the first person I've ever been able to call a friend."

"I won't be the last," he assured me.

"I'm sure you won't be." He seemed to know a lot of the gods and goddesses already, and even had some bonds with them that couldn't be ignored. Perhaps some of them would become my friends in the years to come. It would be interesting to see what happened.

"I don't know what my life would have become if you hadn't had the patience to stay with me for the past few years."

"You'd have found your way. If there's anything I've learned about you, it's that your resourcefulness is only matched by your determination. Even if I hadn't stayed, you'd have been just fine," he said.

"Regardless of that, I'm glad you did."

"Oh, me too." He reached out and cupped my cheek in his hand.

My eyes fluttered closed as I waited for his lips to meet mine, knowing what was coming and welcoming it with everything I had.

I sank into this kiss, feeling his relief and

affection in his every touch. Even if our relationship hadn't become something more, I would be returning alongside him. Knowing I didn't have to face Ra alone was enough.

But this made it better. It gave me a future I'd never imagined possible.

EIGHT

IT LOOKED EXACTLY like I remembered it, but maybe busier. No. That was my imagination. A few years wasn't very much time when it came to the lives of immortal gods.

"It's going to be all right," Thoth promised as we made our way to the entrance.

I nodded, sure he was telling the truth, but nervous all the same. The last time I'd been within the temple walls, I'd been little more than a prisoner. A small part of me worried that would be the case again. I didn't think it would be Thoth who betrayed me, I trusted him with my heart and soul.

Ra, on the other hand...

It was best not to think about it until I was face to face with the sun god. Which would probably happen within minutes of me entering the temple complex.

"You can do this," Thoth assured me.

I plastered a smile on my face. "I hope you're right."

"I'm the god of wisdom, I have to be," he teased.

The two of us made our way inside, the whispers starting among the priests and priestesses the moment they saw us.

The Eye of Ra has returned. They whispered it to one another as if they thought I couldn't hear.

As if I didn't have a name.

Funnily enough, that was all it took for my resolve to deepen. I raised my head and strode through the temple, searching for Ra and waiting for the moment I could finally confront him.

I didn't have to wait long. He strode towards us with a dissatisfied expression on his face. I had no idea if it was aimed at me specifically, or was for Thoth actually managing to bring me back. There was a chance that hadn't been what Ra wanted after all.

"Eye," he addressed me.

"My name is Nehmetawy," I said, making sure I projected my voice as far and wide as I could. The more people heard this, the better my chances of making it stick.

Ra's nostrils flared as he took it all in. "Fine, Nehmetawy. I have tasks for you to perform."

"No."

"What?"

"I refuse to kill. I refuse to attack. I am a goddess in my own right and I won't be used to destroy lives."

Approval and pride flowed off Thoth in waves, but he didn't say anything. This was my moment, and no one was going to take it away from me.

"You've changed," Ra observed.

"No, I haven't. I simply discovered how to use my voice."

Ra's gaze flitted to Thoth with an accusatory glint in it.

"This had nothing to do with Thoth. I made the decision to leave before I even met him." I wasn't going to have someone innocent blamed for this. "The only thing Thoth is responsible for is my return. He convinced me when none of your other messengers even came close."

Ra pursed his lips, displeasure evident on his face. "Fine," he muttered, turning and walking away without another word.

"I see he hasn't improved in the time I've been gone," I muttered.

"Did you really think he would?" Thoth asked.

"No. But I did expect him to put up more of a fight."

"There were a lot of whispers going around before I left to come to you in Punt that he was already working on replacing you with Sekhmet."

"Why didn't you tell me that before?"

"Would it have made a difference?"

I frowned, trying to work out whether or not it would have done. "I don't know."

"And I didn't want you to decide to come back because you knew someone else was doing the job Ra forced you into. You had to decide to come yourself and say it was something you didn't want."

A small smile lifted at my lips. "Thank you. For everything. I thought I felt free in Punt, but that's nothing like I feel now. I get to be me. And I get to find out who that is when I'm surrounded by other people."

"I can't wait to see you grow," he responded.

I reached out and touched his cheek. I pulled away again almost instantly. I had no idea if he wanted other people to see that the two of us were together.

He caught my hand and tugged me close. Our lips collided and he kissed me deeply as he ever had, right in the middle of the temple grounds. I guessed he didn't care who knew about us, then. I was glad about that.

We broke apart, both grinning widely.

"Do you have anywhere to stay here?" he asked.

I shook my head. "I had a room Ra kept me in, but there wasn't any furniture in it, and it was very miserable."

"I expected as much. Let's head to my part of the temple and I'll have some of my priests speak with Ptah about building you one of your own," he said.

"You want to get rid of me that quickly?"

He chuckled. "Not at all. But you need your own space, or how are people going to come worship and serve you?"

I blinked a couple of times. "People serving me?"

"You are a goddess," he pointed out.

"I know, but that hadn't crossed my mind."

"I suspect there are a lot of things that haven't. But I'll be around to help you work through them all," he said.

"Thank you. For everything. For helping me now, for bringing me back, for being my friend, and for more..."

"You've done a lot of that for me too," he promised.

I closed my eyes and let it all sink in. It was hard to believe this was happening. I was at Karnak as a goddess in my own right and not as a tool of Ra's. I had someone by my side who would help me through everything I needed, and I had all the time in the world to discover who I really was.

Things could only look up from here.

THANK you for reading Collector of Sand and Tears, I hope you enjoyed Nehmetawy and Thoth's story. If you want more from the Forgotten Gods: Origins series, you can with Isis and Osiris in Queen Of The Two Lands: http://books2read.com/queenofthetwolands

You can get a free Forgotten Gods short story when you sign up to my newsletter: https://books.authorlauragreenwood.co.uk/7vdbfsavkc

AUTHOR NOTE

Nehmetawy is an interesting goddess in that she's not a very well known one. She's generally considered to have appeared during the New Kingdom, but was most prevalent in the Greco-Egyptian period (Cleopatra's time). She's often associated with being the wife of Thoth when she is remembered, and is sometimes referenced in the myths of the Eye of Ra. The Distant Goddess, the myth I based Collector of Sand and Tears on, is often unclear about which goddess the Eye of Ra becomes. Some say Hathor, some say Sekhmet, others say Nehmetawy and some say yet more goddesses - often claiming they are the same deity. This is probably due to the nature of the Egyptian pantheon where different gods and goddesses had different roles depending where and when in the Egyptian empire they existed.

One reason for me choosing to use the Nehmetawy version of the Distant Goddess myth was that she was also linked to Thoth, and that both Hathor and Sekhmet (the most common goddesses linked to the myth) already exist in my universe as characters, in The Queen Of Gods series and Daughter Of The Sun respectively.

Napata, the city that Nehmetawy is sent to by Ra in the prologue, is commonly thought to be the most Southern settled city during the New Kingdom of Ancient Egyptian history (during which the events of Collector of Sand and Tears is set). The city is real, but it isn't part of the original story. The reason I chose the city is that one of the places the Eye of Ra is said to have run to is the Land of Punt. While no one is completely sure where Punt is, despite it being a notable trader with the Egyptian Empire, Egyptologists believe it was to the south of Egypt and includes part of the Horn of Africa and the Arabian Peninsula.

The story Thoth tells Nehmetawy in chapter 2 is an Egyptian folklore tale called The Princess in the Suit of Leather.

If you want to keep up to date with new releases

and other news, you can join my Facebook Reader Group or mailing list.

Stay safe & happy reading!

- Laura

You can find out more about each of my series on my website.

Obscure Academy

A paranormal romance series set at a university-age academy for mixed supernaturals. Each book follows a different couple.

The Apprentice Of Anubis

An urban fantasy series set in an alternative world where the Ancient Egyptian Empire never fell. It follows a new apprentice to the temple of Anubis as she learns about her new role.

Cauldron Coffee Shop

An urban fantasy series following a witch who discovers a cursed warlock living in a teapot.

The Shifter Season

A paranormal Regency romance series following shifters as they attempt to find their match. Each book follows a different couple.

Forgotten Gods

A paranormal adventure romance series inspired by Egyptian mythology. Each book follows a different Ancient Egyptian goddess.

Amethyst's Wand Shop Mysteries (with Arizona Tape)

An urban fantasy murder mystery series following a witch who teams up with a detective to solve murders. Each book includes a different murder.

Grimm Academy

A fantasy fairy tale academy series. Each book follows a different fairy tale heroine.

Purple Oasis (with Arizona Tape)

A paranormal romance series based at a sanctuary set up after the apocalypse. Each book follows a different couple.

Supernatural Snow Fair

A paranormal romance series based at a Christmas/winter fair. Each book follows a different couple.

Speed Dating With The Denizens Of The Underworld (shared world)

A paranormal romance shared world based on

mythology from around the world. Each book follows a different couple.

Broomstick Bakery

A complete paranormal romance series following a family of witches who run a magical bakery. Each book follows a different couple.

Grimalkin Academy

A complete urban fantasy academy series following a witch cursed to create kittens every time she does magic.

The Paranormal Council

A complete paranormal romance series following paranormals trying to find their fated mates. Each book follows a different couple.

You can find a complete list of all my books on my website:

https://www.authorlauragreenwood.co.uk/p/book-list.html

Signed Paperback & Merchandise:

You can find signed paperbacks, hardcovers, and merchandise based on my series (including stickers, magnets, face masks, and more!) via my website: https://www.authorlauragreenwood.co.uk/p/shop.html

ABOUT LAURA GREENWOOD

Laura is a USA Today Bestselling Author of paranormal, fantasy, urban fantasy, and contemporary romance. When she's not writing, she drinks a lot of tea, tries to resist French macarons, and works towards a diploma in Egyptology. She lives in the UK, where most of her books are set. Laura specialises in quick reads, whether you're looking for a swoonworthy romance for the bath, or an action-packed adventure for your latest journey, you'll find the perfect match amongst her books!

Follow Laura Greenwood

- Website: www.authorlauragreenwood.co.uk
- Mailing List: https://www.authorlauragreenwood.co.uk/p/book-sign-up.html
- Facebook Group: http://facebook.com/groups/theparanormalcouncil

- Facebook Page: http://
  facebook.com/authorlauragreenwood
- Bookbub: www.bookbub.com/authors/
  laura-greenwood